IMAGINE THAT

Licensed exclusively to Imagine That Publishing Ltd
Tide Mill Way, Woodbridge, Suffolk, IP12 1AP, UK
www.imaginethat.com
Copyright © 2022 Imagine That Group Ltd
All rights reserved
0 2 4 6 8 9 7 5 3 1
Manufactured in China

Written by Seb Davey
Illustrated by Vicky Lommatzsch

ISBN 978-1-80105-489-8

A catalogue record for this book is available from the British Library

BLACK & WHITE

Written by
Seb Davey

Illustrated by
Vicky Lommatzsch

Lottie is a **black–and–white** panda and does not like playing with **white–and–black** pandas — they have absolutely nothing in common at all!

Lola is a **white-and-black** panda and does not like playing with **black-and-white** pandas — they have absolutely nothing in common at all!

Lottie loves her mum and dad.

Lola loves her dad and her mum.

Lottie loves sleeping until noon.

Lola loves to get up at midday.

Lottie loves cuddles and snuggles.

Lola loves snuggles and cuddles.

Lottie loves to eat bamboo.

Lola loves to eat bamboo, too!

"I didn't realise that **white-and-black** pandas like to eat bamboo," said Lottie to Lola.

"I didn't realise that **black-and-white** pandas like to eat bamboo either," said Lola to Lottie.

"Maybe there are more things that we both like?" suggested Lottie.

"Maybe," Lola replied.

Lottie and Lola spent the whole day together and discovered they had lots of things in common ...

Lottie and Lola had the best day EVER!

And from that day, Lottie the **black-and-white** panda and Lola the **white-and-black** panda realised that they were not so very different after all.

And they became the very best of friends,

forever.